This edition published exclusively
for Marks and Spencer p.l.c.
by Purnell Books, Paulton, Bristol BS18 5LQ, a member of the
BPCC group of companies

ISBN 0 361 06007 6
'Henry's Cat' copyright © 1983 Bob Godfrey Films Limited and
Stan Hayward
Illustrations copyright © 1983 Bob Godfrey Films Limited and
Stan Hayward
Text copyright © 1983 Purnell Publishers Limited
Published August 1983
Made and printed in Great Britain by Purnell and Sons
(Book Production) Limited, Paulton, Bristol
Third impression

Henry's Cat

By Stan Hayward
Illustrated by Bob Godfrey

St Michael

The Letter

Henry's Cat had overslept. He had dreamt that he had got up and had breakfast, but in spite of eating and eating, he still felt hungry and looked in the cupboard to find there was no food left.

It was a disaster and his worst possible nightmare, so he was very happy to wake up to the sound of his tummy rumbling, and to find he was still hungry but there was

food in the cupboard. He went sleepily downstairs to get breakfast, and on the way, saw a letter on the mat.

It was no ordinary letter. It was in a coloured envelope, so it was obviously something special.

''I expect it is a Christmas card,'' he thought as he stared out the window at the freshly blooming flowers of spring. Then he thought perhaps it was an Easter card, and shook it to see if he could tell by the sound. He couldn't. It was too much for a small cat who had just had a nightmare. He would have to have breakfast first and then open it.

After breakfast of toasted prunes and custard, he opened the letter. It said:

Dear Sir or Madam or Pussycat.
We are happy to inform you that your late Great Aunt Matilda has left you an inheritance under certain conditions that we will discuss. Please come as soon as possible.
Yours faithfully,
Mr Blimp.

Well, this was a surprise. He didn't remember having a
Great Aunt Matilda, but she might have been the one that
lived in Australia or somewhere. It was very nice of her
to think of him, and he would have liked to have met a
great aunt like that. But he would now go and meet her
friend, and that was nearly as good.

The next day, he was all ready to go. He was dressed in his very smartest clothes, and had a large bag to carry all his inheritance back in. He got on the bus and was soon at Mr Blimp's office.

He knocked on the door, and a voice said, ''Who's there?''

''It's Henry's Cat,'' said Henry's Cat.

''Henry's Cat who?'' said Mr Blimp.

''Henry's Cat, Henry's Cat,'' said Henry's Cat.

"Oh yes. Please come in," said Mr Blimp, opening the door. He showed Henry's Cat to a seat.

Mr Blimp looked at Henry's Cat closely through his spectacles, and after studying him for a while said: "Ah, so you are Henry's Cat. Do you have proof of identity like a driving licence, cheque book or something like that?"

Henry's Cat looked in his bag to see if he had something like that. He didn't. He had a small lemon meringue pie, a chocolate cream sausage, a spare

shoelace in case of emergency, and a tin opener in case someone offered him some catfood. He showed these to Mr Blimp, but he didn't think that they were really proof of identity.

Henry's Cat thought about it. He then got up and looked in a mirror on the wall just to check it was him. It was. He pointed this out to Mr Blimp, and also showed him the letter that was addressed to him. Mr Blimp thought that this would be all right, so he continued.

"Well, Henry's Cat, your Great Aunt Matilda was a very generous lady and has left you lots of money . . ."

"I've brought a bag to take it home," said Henry's Cat, butting in rather rudely.

"Yes," said Mr Blimp, "but there are certain conditions that have to be satisfied first. You have to prove that you are a worthy heir to her fortune, otherwise it will go to the Battersea Cats' Home."

Henry's Cat was a bit puzzled by all of this.

"What's a worthy air?" he asked.

"A worthy heir, not a worthy air. You have to prove that you are kind, honest, generous, loyal, and in every way lovable like a true pussycat should be." He closely studied Henry's Cat again, and stroked his chin as if in a little bit of doubt.

"Oh I am. Yes I am, everyone knows that," said Henry's Cat, not in the slightest doubt about it himself.

"I'm sure you are," Mr Blimp sighed. "But you have to prove it. If people point you out and say it and I hear them say it, then, and only then, can I act on behalf of

your Great Aunt Matilda and give you the money.''

It was rather a big problem for a small Cat to solve. Mr Blimp could see that he needed help.

"What I suggest is that you go out and do what you normally do in your village. I will come down and observe you for a day. If I see you acting as a worthy heir then I can give you the money. Does that sound fair?"

Henry's Cat thought it did, so they arranged for Mr Blimp to come down the next day. Henry's Cat went home on the bus, eating his chocolate cream sausage. He offered a bit to the conductor just to get in practice.

The next day, Henry's Cat was all prepared. He was going to do lots of good deeds and be a very worthy heir. The first thing he saw was a lady coming out of a big shop carrying two large bags of groceries. He immediately went up to her and offered to help. She looked round quickly and then said, "That is most kind of you," and gave him a bag. Then she hurried off as fast as she could. Henry's Cat was about to hurry after her when a man from the shop came out and put his hand on Henry's Cat's shoulder.

"Excuse me, sir, do you have a receipt for those goods you are carrying?"

Henry's Cat looked very surprised and said, "Oh no, I was just helping a lady."

"Ah, just helping a lady, were you, so you were her accomplice," said the shopkeeper.

"Oh no," exclaimed Henry's Cat, not knowing what an accomplice was, but sure he wasn't one. "I've never met her before."

"Where is she then?" asked the man, looking around.

There was no lady to be seen. It was a very difficult situation. He thought it best just to give the bag to the man, which he did, and backed away saying, "Sorry to have bothered you."

But as he was backing away, not looking where he was going, he bumped into an old man with a walking stick, and knocked him down. He turned round to help the old man, but first picked up his stick.

The man from the shop thought Henry's Cat was about

to hit him with the stick, and dropped the basket so everything went all over the floor. Other people coming into the shop slipped on the spilt jam and sauce and milk and everything.

The shopkeeper ran away to call the police, and Constable Bulldog arrived very quickly to find Henry's Cat in the middle of a big heap of people and all covered in food.

Constable Bulldog and the shopkeeper took Henry's Cat away to the police station. The next day Henry's Cat had to face the judge who read out the charges.

"You, Henry's Cat, are charged with being an accomplice to a lady who was taking goods without

payment. You also knocked over an elderly man, and
threatened the shopkeeper with a stick, disrupted the
shop and caused confusion among shoppers. This is a
very serious offence for a small cat to commit. Do you
have anything to say for yourself?''

   ''Yes, sir. I was just trying to prove that I am honest,
loyal, helpful, generous, and lovable like a good pussycat
should be,'' said Henry's Cat.

   ''It sounds to me as if you are trying to deceive as
well,'' said the judge. ''I shall have to take that into

account when sentencing you. Are there any witnesses to speak in your defence?"

A voice from the back of the court said, "Yes, here m'lord," and when Henry's Cat turned round, he was surprised to see Mr Blimp.

"I've known Henry's Cat for a long time. He is very generous and helpful, and a good citizen. Why, only yesterday he offered to pay a large sum of money to the Battersea Cats' Home to help those in need," and with that Mr Blimp came forward and showed the judge the cheque.

The judge looked at it, and then at Henry's Cat and said, "Well, I will take that into account and let you go this time, but any more of this hooliganism and I will be more severe next time. Case dismissed," and with that everyone went off to have tea and buns.

Henry's Cat was very grateful to Mr Blimp who explained that he had been watching all the time and understood the mistake, but it is very difficult sometimes to explain to people, so he did the only thing he could do. He was sorry that Henry's Cat had lost all the money, but he would have lots of friends at the Battersea Cats' Home, many who would be very grateful to him and send him Christmas cards every birthday and that sort of thing.

As Henry's Cat thought about all those poor cats mewing in despair because no one loved them, he realised his cheque served a worthy cause, and he was a worthy heir, in spite of not getting the money. The thought pleased him, and he raised his tea saying, "Well, no mews is good mews," and drank their health.

The Cowboy

Henry's Cat rocked back and forth in his rocking chair and shouted "bang bang . . . bang bang!" as he pointed his finger at the TV screen and made out he was chasing bandits. He loved cowboy films and watched every one of them.

When the programme finished, the announcer said, "We have a competition for children everywhere, and that includes pussycats. We will now show you a little bit of an old cowboy film, and you have to guess what film it was, and the names of the cowboys in it.'' Well, Henry's Cat knew everything about the film and immediately wrote it down on a postcard and sent if off.

He completely forgot about the competition until one day a letter arrived.

'Dear Mr Henry's Cat,' it said. 'You have won our cowboy competition, and as a prize you will spend two weeks in America living with real cowboys.'

Well, this was a surprise. Henry's Cat immediately got on his rocking chair and practised horse riding, pretend shooting, and lassoing the coal bucket, just to get into shape. After accidentally lassoing the table lamp and letting it fall into the custard, which then dripped into his bedroom slippers, he decided to wait till he got to America to practise.

The next week he set off on his holiday. It was the very first time he had been on an aeroplane and it was very exciting. He sat next to a little boy who could make car noises while holding his nose. Henry's Cat was very impressed, and took out his water pistol to show him.

"What's your name?" he asked.

"Jack," said the little boy.

"Hi, Jack, I've got a gun," said Henry's Cat.

Well, what a commotion!

The stewardess who was passing shouted, "It's a hijack and he's got a gun!" and put her hands up, which was awkward as she was carrying the dinners, and these went all over the passengers, who then all dived under their seats.

"What's happening?" said Henry's Cat, thinking perhaps it was lifeboat drill.

"It's all right," said Jack, who stood up on his seat and explained everything.

The Captain then came along and spoke to Henry's Cat and said it was very naughty to upset everyone, but as it was his first time on an aeroplane he would forgive him and allow him to come and sit in the cockpit. He allowed

Henry's Cat to hold the steering wheel and steer round
clouds that got in the way.

Soon, Henry's Cat had arrived, and was whisked away
in a big car to a proper ranch where there were real
cowboys and horses and everything.

They gave him a rocking horse to practise on and showed him how to drink a whole glass of lemonade in one go. He was very good at both, and all the cowboys thought him very clever.

The next day they all went out on the range and ate baked beans and sang cowboy songs and told stories of bandits and rustlers, and of the Lone Ranger who was such a good shot that he could hit an acorn tossed in the air with his eyes shut and back turned, while patting his head with one hand and whistling 'My Darling Clementine' — and that wasn't all he could do.

Henry's Cat was very impressed with being a tough cowboy, and almost resolved to have only cold water in his hot-water bottle that night, but just as he was thinking about it, a cowboy rode very fast into the camp.

''The canyon's flooding!'' he hollered. ''Old Zeke is trapped and we've got to get there mighty fast, partners!''

Well, this was no time for cold hot-water bottles. They all got on their horses. Henry's Cat sat behind one cowboy and held on fast while they galloped away shouting "Yahoo" and that sort of thing.

They soon arrived and, sure enough, old Zeke was on a little island in the middle of the river at the bottom of the canyon. He was glad to see everyone and waved his shirt on the end of a stick.

"How are we going to get across the river in time," asked the Head Cowboy. "We haven't got a bridge and we can't swim the river and it's too far to throw a lasso. What are we going to do, eh?"

No one knew what to do. They looked at each other and one suggested they call the fire brigade, but there wasn't a phone handy and time was running out. Well, it was a bother, but Henry's Cat had seen lots of cowboy films and remembered one just like this. He went up to the Head Cowboy.

"Excuse me, Mr Head Cowboy, I've got an idea."

Well, the rest of the cowboys just looked at him and then started laughing, and one said: "Ha ha, the pussycat's got an idea. I expect he'll throw old Zeke a Fe-line, ha ha!"

They all laughed, and Henry's Cat was about to get upset when the Head Cowboy said, "OK, OK, now you all just shut up and listen to this gent pussycat," and they all listened.

"What I would do," said Henry's Cat very seriously, "is this. It's too far for one lasso, but not too far for lots of lassos tied together, so if someone can get to the island

with lots of lassos then old Zeke can be pulled back. As I'm only a small cat, I could float over to the island on a small log and give the lasso to old Zeke."

The Head Cowboy thought about it. "It's a good idea, but we can't pull old Zeke across the river because he can't swim, so we'd better think up something else."

"I've thought of that," said Henry's Cat. "I could give him my hot-water bottle blown up like a life jacket." He took out his hot-water bottle and tied it round him the way they had shown him on the aeroplane.

Well, the Head Cowboy was very impressed.

"Why, bless my soul, I guess you got somethin' there. OK, boys, get started."

They all tied their lassos together just as the cowboys in the old film had done.

It didn't take long to rescue old Zeke — thanks to Henry's Cat. They all said how clever he was, and a real cowboy, and Henry's Cat shrugged and said, ''Aw, it was nothing,'' and stuck his hands in his pockets and pretended he was chewing something.

When they all got back to the ranch, the cowboys told everyone about Henry's Cat's idea.

''Naw, he ain't no Greenhorn, he's a real, rough, tough cowboy, even with a hot-water bottle,'' said the Head Cowboy. ''Give him a double milkshake,'' which they did, and he drank it down in one go, and said:

''Well, a man's got to do what he's got to do, and that goes for pussycats too!'' With that Henry's Cat toddled off to bed feeling that enough's enough . . . even for a pussycat.

The Election

It was a terrible day. Henry's Cat's hot-water bottle had leaked in the night; his tin opener had bent as he tried to open his last tin of catfood, and now . . . his TV wouldn't work. It was the last straw, there is nothing worse for a pussycat than to have a TV that doesn't work. Henry's Cat looked out at the cold, rainy weather and felt very miserable.

"Well, all bad things come in threes, so we've got them over for today," he said to himself, and decided the only thing to do was to visit his friend Chris Rabbit who would cheer him up.

When he got there, he started to tell Chris how miserable he was.

"There should be a law against cats being unhappy," he said, and as he said it, he wondered why no one had thought of passing such a law. It was very inconsiderate of them — whoever they were, and if he were in charge there'd be lots of changes made, that was for sure.

As the thought grew stronger he realised how unfair the world was to those who couldn't defend themselves — like small cats. For example, he was never given free luncheon vouchers or train tickets to the seaside, or gold watches made of chocolate with someone saying: "Thank you for years of faithful service. Will you eat it here or shall we wrap it up?"

What pussycats of the world needed was a strong forceful leader, full of charm and wit; dashing with vitality, full of boundless energy; articulate, magnetic, and able to make instant decisions. In fact, someone just like himself.

The thought of it totally exhausted him, and he got off the table and went to look for Chris Rabbit who had hidden in the cupboard under the sink until Henry's Cat had finished.

Henry's Cat found him and said, "I . . . have decided to stand for Mayor, and I want you to be my publicity manager, and tell everyone that I intend to change things because I've had enough of it all." And with that, Henry's Cat held his head high, and walked out of the house, watched from under the sink by an amazed Chris Rabbit.

When Henry's Cat got home he went up to the TV set, thumped his fist on top and said, "It's all your fault." The TV set immediately started working again after the thump, and the Prime Minister came on giving a speech. This seemed worse than not having it working, so he switched off and went to bed with a tomato sandwich to give him strength for his forthcoming election.

The next day, Henry's Cat and his friends got together to decide how to help him get elected.

Pansy Pig said, "What you have to do is make lots and lots of promises and call other people names. That's what they all do."

And Douglas Dog said, "And you've got to have your picture all over the place saying 'Henry's Cat rules OK' — they all do that."

Then Sammy Snail said, "And you have to knock on doors and tell people you'll give them free lettuce leaves."

Chris Rabbit butted in with, "And free carrots."

And Mosey Mouse butted in, "And free cheese . . ." and they all suggested their own favourite food.

Well, Henry's Cat soon got into practice by promising them all that they would get anything they wanted, provided they voted for him.

Henry's Cat practised hard all week. He watched every speech on TV and tried to copy what they said and did, and then made up a few things of his own till he was very confident. He got his grandfather's top hat and waistcoat and tried them on in front of the mirror. He looked very impressive, and had no doubts about being elected.

The next day was to be his first speech in public. Chris Rabbit had arranged a soapbox near a bus stop where lots of people often stood around doing nothing in particular. Denise Duck and Pansy Pig dressed up as cheer leaders with white boots and banners.

Henry's Cat arrived on his bicycle and leaned it up against the soapbox, then got up and addressed everyone at the bus stop.

"Dear sir or madam. Many of you do not get free luncheon vouchers, or even breakfast and tea-break vouchers. Now is the time to push forward. Give us the gold watches and we will finish the job . . ."

He forgot what came next, but Denise and Pansy came to his rescue by shouting, "One, two, three, four, Henry's Cat will give you more!" Then Denise Duck did a backwards somersault and fell in a puddle.

Henry's Cat then remembered some more of his speech. "Many others offer false promises, that they do not keep, but I will keep my false promises — that I promise."

Everyone by the bus stop started to cheer, but just then the bus came and they all got on, leaving no one except a little girl who explained that she knew how to blow raspberries, and proceeded to demonstrate this.

It had not been the sort of success that Henry's Cat had hoped for. It needed more direct action. He would go directly to the Mayor himself and complain. This he did, with all his friends behind him.

When they got to the Mayor's office, Henry's Cat knocked loudly on the door and then leaned back with his arms folded and put on a very serious expression.

The Mayor — who had been taking his afternoon nap — woke up and came out in his pyjamas. He was very surprised to see Henry's Cat and all his friends, but when he heard what they wanted, he was very sympathetic.

"I know it's very difficult to satisfy everyone. In fact, three old age pensioners were here only yesterday demanding free skateboard lessons as part of their pension. It's very difficult, but I'll tell you what you can do. I'm in the middle of a nap, and I'm supposed to be opening the new village rubbish dump this afternoon. As you are all nicely dressed up, I wonder if you could go along instead and act as assistant Mayor for the

THE TO VILLAGE DUMP

afternoon. You will get free tea and biscuits, plus your
name in the paper, and you can keep any rubbish they
are not using. Does that sound fair?''

Well, Henry's Cat had to admit that it was very fair
indeed, particularly as he had come to complain. So they
all went off to the village rubbish dump, and there it was,
a big hole in the ground, and beside it a truck of rubbish.

His job was to smash a bottle of lemonade against the truck and say, "God bless this rubbish truck and all who sail in her," and then the rubbish would be dumped in the hole and everyone would cheer and have tea and biscuits.

When Henry's Cat explained who he was, everyone gathered round and waited for his speech from on top of a dustbin especially brought for the occasion. He stood on top and addressed the crowd, making up his speech as he went along.

"I have come here today to give you a lot of old rubbish, or at least to give this hole here a lot of old rubbish, and, with this bottle of lemonade, I declare this hole open."

Well, he couldn't have said a truer word. He swung the bottle so hard that it smashed with a great splash and some went in his eyes. He stepped off the dustbin and fell right into the hole. The dustman in the truck heard the smash and pressed the button to tip all the rubbish into the hole.

And I expect you've guessed what happened. It went all over Henry's Cat at the bottom!

Everyone immediately climbed down the hole and started to sort through the rubbish to find Henry's Cat. They soon did. He was covered in fishbones, old rags, and lots of other dustbin things. The photographers thought this was a very good picture and took lots of photos. Henry's Cat had had enough of being Mayor for the day and went home for a bath.

The next day he saw his photo in the paper. He looked just like an old tramp sitting on a throne of rubbish and surrounded by all his friends, also covered in rubbish. It was a very funny sight, except of course to those in the picture. The caption said: **Henry's Cat-astrophe. Vote for him and get free rubbish vouchers.**

Henry's Cat decided that being Mayor would not make him or anyone else any happier. Perhaps he expected too much from life. But then, everything comes to him who waits, and he decided that he had waited long enough for his supper! So he had two helpings of everything just to make up for it.

The Television Advert

It was such a beautiful day that Henry's Cat felt it must be someone's birthday, and a good reason to celebrate. He couldn't think whose birthday it could be, and, after much thought, he decided that perhaps it would come to him later, and he should just get on with celebrating it for the time being.

He wondered what was the right way to celebrate a birthday of someone you haven't thought of yet. It couldn't be a 'For he's a jolly good fellow' sort of birthday or anything like that. It would have to be a sort of sneaking up on it sort of birthday that you celebrate rather quietly by yourself without telling anyone. It needed that sort of food as well — and he had just the thing.

He went to his cupboard and took out a large tin, inside which was a brown cardboard box, inside which was a plastic bag, inside which was a paper wrapper, inside which was a glass jar, inside which was his greatest delight — some Snoggles Special Catfood!

He held it out at arm's length and admired it. Then he took the lid off and closed his eyes as he sniffed it, and let out a long sigh of satisfaction. It was so special that he could not afford it. This had been a Christmas gift that he had saved for just such an occasion.

He put it back in the plastic bag and got ready to go to the park and eat it very slowly with a small spoon and then just lie in the sun with his eyes closed, and say "Happy birthday" to whoever it was. He would have remembered by that time.

He walked around the park looking for just the right seat under a shady tree and with a nice view. He soon found one, and carefully put his bag down and made himself comfortable, then slowly took out his jar of Snoggles Catfood and put it on the seat.

He looked at it and licked his lips, then took the lid off and took his first spoonful . . . mmmmmmmmm, it was so delicious. It was a bit like hot chocolate and cinnamon toast when you've just come in from the cold. On the other hand, it was also a bit like sausage and mash and baked beans when you've been working hard and missed lunch.

Yet again it was similar to the whipped cream that you

can lick from the bottom of your bowl before it is washed. And yet again . . . the more Henry's Cat thought about it the more it seemed similar to all the things he liked, and it was like having them all at once. A beautiful smile spread across his face as he lay back with his eyes closed in the warm sun and said "Happy birthday" to himself.

His blissful state didn't last very long. Someone poked him in the ribs rather hard and Henry's Cat jumped up with a jerk and blinked. There was a man in front of him looking at his Snoggles Catfood. A moment of panic swept over Henry's Cat. Was he being robbed?

But the man, who was wearing dark glasses and smoking a big cigar, smiled, and held his hand out to shake Henry's Cat's paw. With mixed feelings, Henry's Cat held one paw out to be shaken while using the other to hide his catfood behind his back.

"I notice you were eating Snoggles Catfood," said the man, flicking his cigar ash all over Henry's Cat in a nonchalant way. "And you looked so satisfied, I just had to meet you. My name is Bertram B. Sneep, and I advertise Snoggles Catfood on television. I would like you to be in our advert. How do you like that, eh?"

"Oh," said Henry's Cat, not knowing quite what one should say to such a thing.

"And we'll give you a year's supply of Snoggles Special Catfood as a fee. How do you like that, eh?"

Well, a year's supply was quite a lot. It would last him at least two months if he ate with a small spoon, and only on somebody's birthday. It seemed too good an opportunity to miss, and he even started to think that perhaps it was his own birthday.

"Well, here's my card, come and see me tomorrow."

With that the man shook his cigar ash over Henry's Cat once more and then walked off very fast.

Henry's Cat looked at the card. It said: **Bertram B. Sneep, Chief Advertiser of Snoggles Special Catfood.** There was no doubt about it, it had not been a dream. He would soon have a year's supply of Snoggles Catfood all to himself. He quickly ate up the rest of the jar. He had to get into practice.

The next day, Henry's Cat put on his very best bicycle clips and cycled all the way to Mr Sneep's advertising agency.

"You're late," said Mr Sneep. "We'd better get started," and with that he took Henry's Cat into a big studio which had lots of jars and tins of Snoggles Catfood piled up everywhere.

Mr Sneep gave Henry's Cat a script which said "Snoggles Catfood is very good. I always eat it, even when I'm not hungry. It contains vitamin T and vitamin W for healthy tails and whiskers. Get some today!"

"When you've read it, eat some, and then sit back and smile like you did in the park," explained Mr Sneep.

Henry's Cat nodded. It looked very easy, even for a small cat like him. He stood behind a table and started eating the catfood. He was just about half way through and feeling in a blissful mood when Mr Sneep said, "OK, take one," and someone clapped two pieces of board together and the cameras started whirring.

When he had finished, he sat back in his seat and lazily ate the rest of the jar, but Mr Sneep said, "Too long, make it a bit faster. OK, take two,'' and they did it again.

This time Mr Sneep said: ''You missed out vitamin T for healthy tails. OK, take three.''

Well, eating Snoggles Catfood was blissful until the fifteenth try, by which time he was on his seventh jar.

Then it was not quite so blissful, in fact it was a little bit unblissful, so much so that on jar twelve Mr Sneep noticed that Henry's Cat did not have quite the same smile as he had in the park, and complained about it.

"You'll have to give me a few minutes to work up an appetite again," said Henry's Cat, spurred on by the thought of all the catfood he could have, but being out of tummy space.

The next take was just too much. He collapsed in a heap looking rather cross-eyed and holding his tummy. He looked quite ill, and felt even worse. He could just about hear Mr Sneep speaking very angrily, and then suddenly being very happy and saying, "That's it, that's it! OK, all go home."

Henry's Cat didn't remember much more, but woke up next day in hospital, where he had been all night just for

a check. He was fine now and allowed to go home, but the doctors advised him not to eat too much.

When he arrived home he found a big box of Snoggles Catfood waiting outside his door. He couldn't face it, so he hurried in and switched on the TV to forget yesterday.

He had hardly switched on when the adverts started. Of

all the things it had to be an advert for Snoggles Catfood!
Mr Sneep came on and said, "Why look like this?" —
pointing to a very sick-looking Henry's Cat laying on the
floor — "When you can be a healthy, fit cat by eating
Snoggles Catfood" and he held up a jar with a picture of a
smiling cat on it.

Just the sight of more Snoggles Catfood made Henry's Cat feel very ill indeed. He clutched his tummy and said "uurrgghhhh uk!" and closed his eyes.

It was then he remembered whose birthday he had
been celebrating. It was Napoleon's, and he also
remembered what Napoleon had said. It was: "An army
marches on its stomach." Very apt, thought Henry's Cat,
as he lay on his stomach and slowly crawled his way to
bed for the rest of the day, hoping very much that he
wouldn't dream about Snoggles Catfood.

The Photographer

Crash! bang! wallop! thud! plop! . . .
Henry's Cat didn't know what had
happened or what had hit him. All
he knew was that he was sitting on the pavement in a
rather awkward way with egg yolk running down his
face; teabags in his lap; custard powder all over his
knees, and two sticky buns stuck to him.

He looked around rather dazed. There was a sudden
flash before his eyes, then someone helped him up and
asked how he was, and he realised he had been in an
accident. It seemed that a car had come around the
corner and honked its horn, which scared a man on a
bike, who then bumped into a lady with some shopping,
who then tipped her shopping basket over Henry's Cat.

The lady allowed Henry's Cat to keep the two sticky buns just to cheer him up, and then pointed him in the direction of his home. He wobbled his way home and arrived still a little bit dazed. It took both the sticky buns and quite a few more to calm his nerves.

"There should be a law against people honking horns and knocking cats over," he thought to himself, and gave himself a thorough examination in case he had any hidden bruises or more sticky buns. He hadn't any of either so, with mixed feelings of relief and disappointment, he went to bed.

The next day his friend Chris Rabbit arrived early and knocked frantically on his door. Henry's Cat went down in his pyjamas and opened the door. Chris Rabbit waved the local newspaper at him and said in a frantic way:

"I've seen you in the paper!"

He showed Henry's Cat a photo of himself sitting on the pavement with egg all down his face. It was not the best photo he had seen of himself, but it did say underneath the picture: **Innocent bystander run down by mad motorist. Unknown cat suffers two cracked eggs and torn teabag, with multiple sticky buns of the chest, and suspected custard powder under the arms.**

It was obviously very serious, and Henry's Cat wondered why no one had told him how serious it had been. It then occurred to him that the flash before his eyes had been a photographer taking his picture.

"Well, at least it will make people aware that mad motorists are around, and that will help to make a law against them," said Henry's Cat, feeling almost pleased that he had helped. And as the thought grew stronger, it occurred to him that he might become a photographer and take photos that would help make the world a better place for cats to live in — and people as well, of course — but cats didn't drive cars at people nearly as often.

He immediately went up to his attic and looked in his grandfather's trunk. There was a rather large camera there, and with a big tripod and a black cloth that you put over yourself. If was a bit old fashioned, but good enough to start with, he thought. He didn't have any film, but he could practise without that and get some later.

All he needed now was to find some accidents. He realised that they are not usually easy to find until it's too late. Perhaps he could just ask people if they intended having an accident today and then stay with them till it happened.

On the other hand, he could put his camera up at a suitable spot and have a notice saying: **Please have your accident here**. But then it depended on what sort of accident they intended having. He didn't want a 'runaway steamroller' sort of accident, but on the other hand a 'slipping on a banana skin' was quite all right. Then again, he didn't want a 'What's all this then?' from a policeman sort of accident. The 'Are you all right, dear?' sort would be better.

It was while pondering such things and walking along with his camera over his shoulder, that Henry's Cat became aware of a great commotion. His sixth sense told him that this could be an accident.

He looked up and saw a crowd of people by two barrows. One sold hot dogs and the other sold ice cream. The men who owned them were having a big argument about whose barrow should be there.

Henry's Cat quietly set up his camera and put the black cloth over his head. It did not take long for the accident to happen. First the ice-cream man got very angry and threw a scoop of raspberry ice cream at the hot-dog man, who then squirted mustard over the ice-cream man. The hot-dog man threw a bun filled with sliced onions, and the ice-cream man retaliated with a lemon ice lolly. The accident was due any moment now, thought Henry's Cat, as he waited with his finger on the button.

The accident did happen. Constable Bulldog arrived and said, "What's all this then?" and was unlucky enough to get a scoop of vanilla ice cream right in the eye, followed by two hot dogs and a tomato. In the rush to get away quickly, Henry's Cat got knocked down.

He staggered to his feet with the black cloth still over his head, unable to see. He walked right off the pavement and into the road. A car swerved to miss him and crashed into the ice-cream barrow, which knocked the hot-dog barrow and they both overturned in the road. Cars swerved and stopped everywhere as Henry's Cat walked right down the middle of the road trying to get the cloth off his head.

Constable Bulldog couldn't see for ice cream and tomato, and everyone else had disappeared as fast as they could — that is, everyone except a passing photographer who saw his chance to take a photo of an accident.

Luckily Henry's Cat got across the road, and took the cloth off. He saw all the mess, but did not know that he had caused it.

''Oh, what a pity, that's just the sort of picture I was looking for,'' he said. He tucked his cloth under his arm and collected his camera, thinking how unlucky it was that he didn't have a film.

The next day he opened the newspaper and saw himself

again. This time he was a hooded figure staggering across the road with mess everywhere. The headline said: **Maniac cat causes havoc in high street. Reward for information. Have you seen this cat?** Well, luckily there was not much to see, except his feet sticking out of the hood.

Henry's Cat realised that he had caused the accident, and that they were looking for him.

"Oh dear, in this case no news is certainly good news," he said, and pulled all the curtains before creeping up to bed and hiding under the bedclothes for the rest of the day.